RAGS
An Orphan of the Storm
and Other Animal Stories

© 2020 Jenny Phillips

goodandbeautiful.com

Cover design and illustration by Elle Staples

Contents

RAGS

An Orphan of the Storm

Ruth Cromer Weir

Rags: An Orphan of the Storm

by Ruth Cromer Weir

Illustrations by Alice J. Montgomery

Originally published in 1947

Rags: An Orphan of the Storm

"Here's an orphan!" The policeman had to shout above the noise of the thunder. A light twinkled on in the big oak tree at Orphans of the Storm. A hundred dogs began to bark. But the gray puppy did not notice. He was so hungry—and so tired—and so scared!

The policeman's raincoat was wet, and the puppy shivered. There was the sound of quick steps. The little dog heard friendly voices.

"Found him shivering against a building," the policeman said.

"On a night like this!" the manager of the orphanage exclaimed.

"Abandoned!" the policeman went on.

There was another big clap of thunder, and the puppy tried to crawl under the policeman's raincoat. But there was no room there for the wet little dog. The policeman filled up his raincoat himself.

"Looks like a bundle of rags," he said, holding out the shivering little dog. The puppy's fur was wet and matted. He was so hungry and scared that he cried a little.

"You said RAGS? That's what we'll call him," said the manager. "We like to give the dog a name the first thing."

Then Rags was in a small pen. He was drinking warm milk. He drank and drank. At last he was satisfied. He licked his whiskers. He yawned.

When he awoke, the sun was shining. Rags looked down a long hall. As far as he could see, there were more pens just like his.

A big dog across the hall saw Rags. "WOOF! WOOF!" he barked.

Then all the other dogs in all the other pens barked, too. There were all kinds of barks from all kinds of dogs. Rags scurried to the corner of his pen and tried to hide.

Rags found that an orphanage for dogs is a very busy place. First the dogs were fed. Each had his own pan of food. Rags was so hungry that he licked his pan clean.

Then the other dogs were taken outside. They exercised in a gravel runway while their pens were scrubbed. When the attendant was not looking, Rags peeked out and watched him. But as soon as the attendant spoke to him, he ran into his corner.

Rags fell asleep after breakfast. Sometime

later, he drew back in fright as someone touched him.

"Didn't you ever have anyone pet you before?" asked the manager. She lifted him gently into her arms. "What you need is a good scrubbing," she said.

She carried him down the hall while the dogs barked on both sides of them. Rags trembled. The woman petted him again. This time he liked it. Somehow, Rags knew that he had found a friend.

His new friend took him into a big room.

It looked like a kitchen, but it had a bathtub instead of a sink. She set him on a white table. Then she started to comb his fur. Rags' fur was tangled. The comb pulled, and he began to whimper.

"Look out the window," she said. "Then it won't hurt so much."

Snip-snip-snip went the scissors. Whenever the manager found a big tangle, she cut it in the middle and made two small tangles. These did not pull so much.

At last she finished combing him. But his hair looked dull. And there were places on him that did not have any hair at all.

Rags shivered when the woman set him in the middle of the big tub. Then she started rubbing his back. It felt so good that he shut his eyes. He sighed a contented sigh as if to say, "Please keep on rubbing."

Rags stuck his nose in the suds. Then he sneezed. And there on the end of his nose was a big soap bubble. Rags shook his head once. Then he shook it again. But the bubble stayed. Then all of a sudden, it POPPED! Rags was so scared, he nearly jumped out of the tub.

"What? Afraid of a soap bubble?" the manager said.

The dirt kept coming out and coming out. Finally, the woman set Rags down on the floor.

He shook and shook. He shook water all over her pretty blue slacks, but she did not seem to mind.

She wiped him dry with a big white towel.

"Look what a bath did," she said happily. "Now you're a beautiful white cairn!"

Imagine Rags' surprise when he looked down. His fur had turned blue-gray and white.

"The next thing we must do is to find a HOME for you," the woman said.

From the way she said it, Rags knew that a home must be something very special. He wagged his tail.

He was taken to a pen at the end of the hall. For the next ten days, Rags was kept in quarantine, away from the other dogs, until the manager could be sure he was in good health. Then one day she let him out.

"You're going to have the run of the place," she said, as she gave Rags a friendly pat. "See if you can get over being so scared." Rags stopped. He saw a boy and his mother.

"Oh, Mom, not *that* dog! The spaniel outside," the boy said.

Rags hung his head. He watched from between two locks of fur as the adoption papers for Skipper, the spaniel, were filled out.

Then the boy rushed to Skipper's kennel in the yard. The spaniel was as excited as the boy.

Rags watched Skipper race to the gate with his new master. He felt lonely and neglected.

After that, he saw many dogs leave the orphanage. People came looking, looking, every afternoon. Some people took dogs home with them.

The dogs seemed to want to be adopted. They barked and begged. Some of them showed off when people came. But Rags did not. He hid under his bench in the corner of his pen.

One day Rags watched Mitzi, a part Pekingese, leave. She ran down the walk with a little girl. After she had gone, Rags ran down the walk to the gate. He pressed his nose against the fence. He looked down the winding road. He wanted to go down the road, too. But no one seemed to want him.

Not long after that, a woman stopped in front of his pen. "This one's cute," she said.

Rags pricked up his ears.

"But I couldn't stand those long hairs on my rugs," she added. Rags' tail went limp.

"Hello there, Ragamuffin," the manager said when she came one day, and Rags jumped happily on her. "What you need is someone to love you all the time. We must find a home for you."

Just then a man came through the office door. "I want a dog," he said. He looked at Rags. "That one wouldn't eat much. I'll take him."

"We don't usually judge a dog by how little he eats," the manager said. "That little dog has a sweet disposition."

Rags' tail brushed the floor as he caught her tone of approval.

"But he is very timid," she continued. "He hasn't had much love. For that reason perhaps he needs even more attention than other dogs.

"Have you ever had a dog?" the manager asked.

"Sure," the man said.

"What happened to him?"

"Oh, we moved. And there wasn't room in the car. And—"

"—And so you did the meanest thing you could do to a dog. You abandoned him. Perhaps he is waiting where you left him. He is hungry and lonely and frightened. But he would still give his very life for *you*."

The man's face turned red. "Listen, lady," he said, "I didn't come to be lectured. I just came to get a dog."

Rags looked up out of the corner of his eye. He crept quietly to the door.

The manager's eyes were sparkling. "You'll not get a dog from Orphans of the Storm," she said.

The man grabbed his hat and started for the door. In his haste, he stumbled over Rags, and they both rolled down the steps.

Baloney and Snowball and Blackie, the friendliest dogs in the orphanage, were standing outside and

pounced on the man. They wanted to play.
They licked his face.

Finally he got away from them. But he was
in such a hurry that he did not wait to see
if the gate was unlocked. He dashed for the
high cyclone fence. As he scrambled over the
wires, his coattail caught on the top. He hung
there. He waved his arms and legs.

Then *RIP-RIP*! *TEAR-TEAR*! He fell to the
ground on the other side of the fence. All the
dogs barked. Rags barked, too. The man ran
away as fast as he could.

The next morning, some children came to visit. Rags had never heard so much noise. He was more scared than ever. He hid under his bench.

The dogs yipped and barked. They stood on their hind legs. They whined and begged to be petted.

The children laughed and shouted.

"Look at Snowball," yelled one.

"I'll take Baloney," said another, and all the children laughed.

Rags heard a whisper. "Hello, doggy!"

Peeking out from under his bench, he saw a little girl with brown pigtails. Her eyes were as blue as her hair ribbons. She looked almost as scared as Rags felt.

Rags crawled from under his bench.

"Come on, Ann," called the others, as they rushed down the hall.

But the little girl knelt before Rags' pen. "Here, doggy!" she said.

Rags' tail started wagging. He moved

towards Ann. But the other
dogs wanted Ann to pet them,
too. They set up a terrible racket. Rags
dashed back to his corner and peeked out
from behind a lock of fur.

Ann brushed her hair back so that she
could see him better.

"I want to pet you," she said.

Rags came slowly towards her. He put

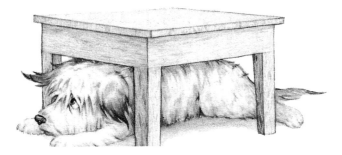

his nose between the wires. Ann touched it gently. He opened his mouth to lick her hand.

"Oh-h-h!" Ann squealed and pulled her hand away. She ran down the hall. Rags went back into his corner. He had tried to be friendly. What could be wrong?

That afternoon some of the children came

back with their mothers. Baloney, Blackie,
and Snowball were adopted.

When Rags heard the children's voices, he
barked. Perhaps Ann had come back for him.
He tried to climb the wire of his pen. Two
bright eyes shone through his long hair as
he watched the door at the end of the hall.
Two little pointed ears fringed in long gray
fur stood straight up as he listened. Now and
then he wagged his tail.

The last of the children left. Rags waited

and waited, but Ann did not come. His tail stopped wagging. His ears dropped. His eyes were not so bright. He climbed slowly down from the wire and curled up in his corner. He buried his face between his front paws.

Suddenly he pricked up his ears.

He crawled out and jumped up on the wire.

He barked—sharp, happy little barks.

"He's down this way, Daddy," he heard Ann say. And there she was, tugging at her father's hand.

Rags was so happy he forgot to be

afraid. Ann was not afraid either. She poked
her fingers through the wire and let Rags lick
them.

"He's yours, Ann," said her father when he
came back a little later to let Rags out of his
pen. "We know you'll love and care for your
adopted dog."

When Ann skipped down
the walk of Orphans of
the Storm, Rags could not
skip. He just hopped and

bounced. But he reached the gate first!

A month after Rags left Orphans of the

Storm, an inspector came to see if he was happy in his new home.

"He's not even scared anymore," Ann told the inspector. "He's not even scared of the big dog down the street.

"I'm not scared either. Daddy says it's because I have Rags. I guess we both like being loved." She picked up the cairn and hugged him.

Rags tugged at one of her pigtails. He wanted to play.

Looking for LUCY

Jane Quigg

Originally published as *Looking for Lucky*

by Jane Quigg

Illustrations by Connie Moran

Originally published in 1946

Looking for Lucy

Tommy Barton had two kittens named Lucy and Happy. Happy was all black. There was not a white hair on him, not even on the tip of his tail. And because the other kitten had a small white spot about as big as a dime right under her chin, so that Tommy could tell them apart, he had named her Lucy. Except for the white spot, Lucy was all black, too.

Lucy and Happy always had their meals together. They drank their milk out of the same saucer and ate their food from the same plate. They were always hungry because they were so young.

Happy was a good kitten. He never went far from home. Lucy often ran away, and sometimes she got lost, but somehow she always was back at mealtime.

One morning when Tommy brought their saucer and the bottle of milk out on the porch to feed them, Happy was there, but Lucy did not appear. Tommy poured out the milk for Happy and took the bottle back into the kitchen. Then he went into the backyard, calling, "Lucy, Lucy!" and looking in his yard and in the neighbors' yards on both sides of his own. But he could not find Lucy.

"I must keep on looking for Lucy," said Tommy. He got on his tricycle and rode here and there and everywhere, calling, "Lucy, Lucy!" as he rode along.

But he could not find Lucy.

Tommy went home, and Mother helped him make a sign and fasten it to the big maple tree in front of his yard. This is what the sign said: *Lucy is lost. Reward offered.*

Tommy went upstairs to his room and picked up four toys to use as rewards for any children who might help him find Lucy. He wanted to give them their choice. Then

Tommy said, "I will get on my tricycle and try again." As Tommy rode along on his tricycle, looking everywhere, he met the postman.

"Hello, Tommy," said

the postman. "No mail for you today."

"I am not looking for mail today," said Tommy. "I am looking for Lucy. Have you seen her?"

"No," said the postman, "but I will keep my eyes open."

"Thank you," said Tommy, riding away.

A little farther on, Tommy met Mr. Benjamin Brewster. Mr. Brewster was very tall, and Tommy had to look up when he talked to him.

"Mr. Brewster," said Tommy, "I have lost Lucy."

"Which kitten is she? The one that is all black?" asked Mr. Brewster.

"No," said Tommy. "It is the one with the white spot about as big as a dime under her chin."

"I will send her to you if I meet her," said Mr. Brewster.

"Thank you," said Tommy.

On the way home, Tommy stopped to rest in Amy Lou's backyard. Amy Lou was playing in her sandbox.

"I am looking for Lucy," said Tommy. "She is lost again."

"When she comes back, I will let you tie her to my beach umbrella," said Amy Lou, "if you like. It is almost always cool under the umbrella."

"Thank you," said Tommy. "But kittens do not like to be tied up. She ought to stay at home with Happy. Cook says to put butter on her paws. That will make her stay home."

"Why will that make her stay home?" asked Amy Lou.

"Because cats like butter, and she could lick it off. Then she would like to stay where she could get butter," said Tommy. "I had better go on home now. Maybe someone has brought her back."

When he was almost home, he saw Peggy,

the little girl from next door, sitting on the bench under the big maple tree in his front yard. She was holding a kitten on her lap. Tommy rode faster. Soon he was in his yard.

"I have found Lucy," called Peggy.

"Good!" said Tommy. "I am glad." He took one look at the little kitten and then said, "Oh, but that one is not Lucy. That is Happy. Lucy is the one with the white spot under her chin."

"Oh dear me!" said Peggy. She put Happy down on the ground, and he started off toward the backyard. "He was on my back porch, and I thought he was Lucy," she said.

"Never mind," said Tommy. "We shall find her all right. It is hard to tell them apart. Anyway, you tried to help me find Lucy, and I am going to give you a reward."

Tommy fished into his right-hand coat pocket and drew out a beautiful red fire engine and put it down on the bench. Then he reached into the left-hand pocket of his coat and pulled out a little green truck and another little yellow roadster. He put them both on the bench. Then he reached into his handkerchief pocket and took out a little silver airplane and put it on the bench beside the others. "Which one do you want?" he asked.

"They are all good things to play with," said Peggy. "I do not know which one to take."

"You had better shut your eyes and say, 'Eeny, meeny, miney, mo.'"

So Peggy shut her eyes and said, "Eeny, meeny, miney, mo," and when she said "mo," she touched the little yellow roadster.

Peggy went home and took the little yellow roadster home with her, and Tommy went to the house to eat his lunch. While he was eating lunch, the doorbell rang. Tommy went to the door, and there stood Freddy Mitchell, whose backyard was just over the fence from Tommy's. Freddy was carrying a

basket. "I have Lucy in here," he said. "I am holding the cover down tight so she cannot get away. I found her in my wagon in our yard."

"Let me see her," said Tommy. "Is she all right?"

Freddy took off the cover, and Tommy looked at the little black kitten. "That is not Lucy," he said. "That is Happy. Happy does not have a white spot under his chin."

Then he took Happy out of the basket and said, "Poor Happy! Everyone thinks you are Lucy."

"Oh," said Freddy.

"Happy is a good cat," said Tommy. "He always comes home by himself unless someone brings him." And Tommy told Freddy that the little girl next door had picked up Happy, too, thinking he was Lucy.

Freddy laughed and said, "Poor Happy!" and patted him. Then Freddy said goodbye and started to walk away.

"Wait a minute," said Tommy. "I want to give you something for trying to find Lucy." He took the little red fire engine, the little green truck, and the little silver airplane from his pockets and said, "Which will you have?"

"I like them all," said Freddy.

"You had better shut your eyes and say, 'Eeny, meeny, miney, mo,'" said Tommy.

Freddy said, "Eeny, meeny, miney, mo," and when he said "mo," he was touching the fire engine. Then Freddy went home and took the little red fire engine with him.

Tommy went back into the house. Happy went with

him, and Tommy filled the kittens' saucer with milk. Happy quickly lapped it all up with his little pink tongue. "Poor little Lucy!" said Tommy. "She must be hungry. I wish she were here, too."

A few minutes later, Tommy telephoned Daddy at his office and told him that Lucy was lost. Daddy promised to come home early to help look for her.

Then Tommy said, "Mother, I think I will get on my tricycle and go and look for Lucy again."

"Don't you think you had better take a rest?" said Mother.

"Not now, please," said Tommy. "I feel as if I ought to keep on looking and looking."

"All right," said Mother. "I hope you find her soon."

Tommy got on his tricycle once more and rode down South Main Street as far as Pelham Road, and up Pelham Road as far as Woodrow Street, and up Woodrow Street until he came to Ellsworth Road, and down Ellsworth Road to South Main Street, and then down South Main Street toward home. He looked in every yard and on every porch but did not see any kitten that looked like

Lucy. Three houses from home, he saw the twins, Dick and Dan, playing in their yard.

"Hello, Tommy," called Dick and Dan. "We have found Lucy!"

Tommy got off his tricycle and ran into the yard. Sure enough, Dick was holding a little black kitten. Tommy took one look at the little black kitten and shook his head.

"Isn't it Lucy?" asked Dick.

"No," said Tommy. "That is Happy. Lucy has a small white spot about as big as a dime under her chin."

"We had to run fast to catch him," said Dick.

"It took us a long time," said Dan.

"Never mind," said Tommy. Then he told

Dick and Dan how Peggy and Freddy had made the same mistake. Dick and Dan smiled. Then they laughed.

"You both deserve a reward just the same," said Tommy. He took the little green truck and the little silver airplane from his pocket. "You may each have one of these," he said.

"I like airplanes," said Dick.

"I like trucks," said Dan.

Tommy gave the little silver airplane to Dick and the little green truck to Dan. "Goodbye," he said. "I am going home to see if Lucy has come back."

When Tommy got home, Lucy was not there. Tommy told his mother that he must change the sign. Mother helped him make a new sign. The new one looked like this:

LOST

A LITTLE BLACK KITTEN

with a

white spot about

AS BIG AS A DIME

UNDER HER CHIN

Reward

Then Tommy sat down on the bench under the big maple tree. He wondered what he could give for a reward this time! He wished that he had more little toys, but he had given away all he had. He would have to give his new sailboat or his new bag of marbles. First, he thought he would give the sailboat. Then, he thought he would give the bag of marbles. At last, he said to himself, "I will let whoever brings Lucy home choose for himself."

It was a hot day. Tommy was tired. He lay down on the bench and soon fell asleep. He slept for a long time in the shade of the maple tree. At last, Tommy felt something soft and furry rubbing against his cheek. He opened his eyes. Happy was cuddled up close to him, purring contentedly.

"Hello, Happy!" said Tommy, sitting up

quickly. "It is time I woke up. Daddy will be home before long. It is time to open the garage doors for him. He is going to help me look for Lucy."

Tommy
walked back

to the backyard, and Happy followed him. Tommy opened the garage door. Then he looked in, and when he did, he could hardly believe his eyes. There stood Lucy!

"Me-ow!" said Lucy.

Tommy picked Lucy up in his arms. "You poor kitten!" he said softly. Lucy began to purr.

Then Tommy took Happy up in his arms with Lucy and carried both kittens into the house to show Mother. When Mother heard where Tommy had found Lucy, she laughed, and said, "Wait until we tell Daddy! When he hears that he locked Lucy in when he closed the garage this morning, he will be surprised."

Then Mother got the kittens' saucer and a bottle of milk, and Tommy poured the milk into the saucer. Lucy stuck her head into the saucer so fast that Tommy spilled some of the milk on her nose.

Happy ran right over to the saucer and stuck his nose in beside Lucy's. Tommy poured more milk into the saucer. He watched the kittens lapping up the milk until the dish was quite empty.

When Lucy looked up, Tommy said, "I am glad that you were not really lost, after all. The next time you are not here at mealtime, I will look for you in the garage, or under the porch, or up in a tree in the yard before I put a sign up. Now I am going to get on my tricycle and tell all the neighbors that I found you."

But before he went, Tommy held Lucy and Happy in his arms for a little while. Both kittens purred and purred.

A House for

LEANDER

Rebecca K. Sprinkle

A House for Leander

by Rebecca K. Sprinkle

Illustrations by Maurice W. Robertson

Originally published in 1953

A House for Leander

On a bright July morning, Peter Tompkins was mowing the lawn. But he was not thinking of the whirring lawn mower. He was not thinking of the sweet smell of cut grass. He was thinking of his Special Wish—his Special Wish for a dog of his very own.

Peter was thinking so hard that he did not hear a truck pull up in front of the house.

"Hi!"

Peter jumped. Then he saw it was Mr.

Flynn, who brought eggs and vegetables
from the country.

"How many eggs does your mom want
today?"

"I'll see!" Peter started for the kitchen.

"Three dozen," Mother decided. She picked
up her big market basket and hurried out
the door. "And I do hope he has some of that
good sweet corn," she added.

"I have," Mr. Flynn called out from the back of the truck. "And tomatoes and beans. And besides all that," he smiled, "I have a dog for Peter!"

For a moment, Peter stood very still. He did not say a word. He could hardly believe his ears. His Special Wish was coming true! Mr. Flynn had a dog for him!

Peter edged over to the truck. He peeked inside. Sure enough, there, tucked in between the baskets of tomatoes and beans, was a dog. It was brown, and it looked as big as a lion.

Mr. Flynn reached in and picked up a leash. He spoke softly. "Come on, boy!" The big animal stood up lazily, stretched slowly, then jumped down in one easy leap.

"Gracious!" Mother stepped back in alarm. "He's huge!"

"He's beautiful!" Peter's eyes glowed. "He's just beautiful!"

Peter stretched out his closed hand for the big dog to sniff. The brown eyes turned to Peter. The dog's long tail thrashed back and forth in friendly greeting.

"He's yours if you want him," Mr. Flynn said.

"That is, if your mother will let you keep him."

"Oh, dear," Mrs. Tompkins sighed. "Do I have to decide this morning?"

"I'm afraid so," Mr. Flynn replied. "If you don't want Peter to have him, I know another family that will take him. He needs a good home."

Peter did not dare speak. He put his arms around the big dog's neck. He rubbed his cheek against the dog's smooth coat.

"There are two things you ought to know." Mr. Flynn leaned against the truck and spoke slowly. "This dog is a big eater. You'd be surprised how much food he can eat in a day."

"Well, the food isn't a special problem." Mother was almost talking to herself. "Peter's grandfather runs a store. He offered to supply the food if Peter ever had a dog."

"The other thing you should know," Mr. Flynn went on, "is that this dog is named Leander. He has had that name since he was a puppy. He's too old to learn a new one. You'll have to call him Leander, whether you like the name or not."

"Leander!" Peter said it under his breath. "That's a good name for a big dog."

"I rather like the name Leander, too,"

Mother said. She thought for another moment. Then she turned to Peter. "But there's one thing," she declared firmly. "He won't be allowed to sleep in the house. He's too big."

"Will you agree to that, Peter?" Mr. Flynn looked straight at Peter.

"Oh, sure!" Peter said. His arms were still around Leander. "I guess he could sleep in the garage."

"You and Daddy will have to work that out," said Mother. "But I just can't have him in the house."

Peter took the leash. He still could not believe that it was true. Leander was to be his!

"Oh, thank you!" he called out as Mr. Flynn climbed into the truck.

"Have fun with Leander!" Mr. Flynn called back.

Peter pulled his big wagon down to
Grandfather's store. Grandfather loaded the
wagon with two sacks of dog food, and Peter
pulled it home.

The rest of the day went by like a happy
dream. Leander was a fine companion. The
Parker twins who lived next door came over
to see him. They played ball in the backyard.
Leander played, too. He chased the ball and

telephone rang. When Daddy came back, he said, "It was Mr. Parker. He offered us their old doghouse."

"Let's try it for Leander!" Peter exclaimed.

"Maybe then he would be happy," Mother said.

During the day two men brought over the doghouse. The twins came along and stayed to play with Peter and Leander.

"I hope this will be right for Leander," Daddy said that evening.

Peter put the soft old blanket into the doghouse. The big dog sniffed it over in his slow, careful way. Then he eased his big body into the house.

Daddy and Peter saw at once that the Parkers' doghouse would not do. When Leander stretched out, almost half of his body was outside!

"This dog needs something special," said Daddy. "He needs something built just for him."

"The way our house was built just for us?" Peter asked.

"You're right, Peter," Daddy agreed. "We were blessed to have someone right in the family who knows all about planning houses for people—an architect. Uncle Jim planned this house especially for us."

"Maybe Leander needs an architect, too," Peter giggled. "Do you think Uncle Jim would plan a house for Leander?"

"Why don't you ask him tomorrow?" said Daddy.

At breakfast Peter told Mother of the plan.

"Why," she said, "that's a good idea! Before he planned our house, Uncle Jim had to know a great deal about all of us and the way we live. Then he knew how to plan a house that would be right for us. Now, Peter, you should be able to tell Uncle Jim all about Leander. Then he will know what kind of house Leander needs."

"I think I can!"

Peter thought a moment. "Leander is big,"

he said. "His house must be big enough to let him stretch out as far as he wants." Mother nodded.

Peter thought again. "Leander loves to thump his tail when he's going to sleep," he said. "And that takes room, because his tail is so long. The house ought to have enough room in the back for him to thump his tail." Mother and Daddy agreed.

Peter thought some more. "When he's tired of playing with the twins and me, he likes to lie in the shade and watch us. But he doesn't like to get the sun in his eyes."

"Sounds as if he needs a porch on his house," chuckled Daddy.

"I believe an architect could help Leander," Mother declared. "It's an architect's job to plan a house that is just right for the ones who will live in it. For a small family, he plans a little house. If it's a big family, he plans a big house with plenty of rooms. Leander is such a big dog that he needs a special doghouse. It should be planned to fit him."

"Uncle Jim may not have time to bother with a doghouse," Daddy warned Peter.

"I'll go to his office and ask him," Peter said.

"Why not take Leander along?" suggested Mother. "Uncle Jim should see your dog before he plans a house for him."

Right after breakfast Peter brushed Leander until his coat shone. Peter washed his own face and brushed his hair until he shone, too. Then he put Leander's leash on him, and they started for Uncle Jim's office.

When Uncle Jim saw Leander, he gave a long whistle. "I like your dog!" he said to Peter.

"Will you plan a house for him?" Peter asked. "He needs a special house because he's so big!"

"I'll be delighted to plan a house for your dog!" Uncle Jim said. "Let me make some notes."

Leander circled around once, twice, three times. Then he flopped in a great heap on the floor.

Peter sat down beside Uncle Jim. He told him all about Leander. Uncle Jim made notes on a piece of paper.

Peter told him that Leander liked to thump his tail just before he went to sleep. He told

him that Leander liked to watch the children play without getting sun in his eyes. He told him that Leander didn't like too big a room because it made him feel lonesome at night.

Uncle Jim looked at the notes he had made. Then he stooped down beside Leander, asleep on the cool floor, and measured him. He found out just how much space the big dog would need. He wrote down some figures. Then he measured Leander's tail. He wrote down that figure, too.

At last he said, "Peter, I will have a plan ready for Leander's house day after tomorrow. It will be a real blueprint, just like the ones I make for big houses."

Peter grinned.

"Your mother has invited me over for

supper that night," Uncle Jim said. "I'll bring the blueprint with me."

Peter and Leander raced all the way home. Peter told Mother about his talk with Uncle Jim. That night, he told Daddy. "I can hardly wait till the day after tomorrow," Peter said.

Mother and Daddy said they could hardly wait, too.

The next day, Peter and Leander and the Parker twins had a ball game in the backyard. When they were tired, they sat in the shade and talked about Leander's new house.

"What will it be like?" the twins asked.

"I don't know yet," Peter answered. "But it will be planned just for Leander."

"I hope Leander will like it," one of the twins said.

Leander lay beside Peter on the grass. He thumped his long tail. The children laughed. It seemed as if he knew about the plans for his new house.

"I can hardly wait to see Uncle Jim's blueprint," Peter said. "It will show just how Leander's house will look."

That night, Mother let Leander sleep
in the kitchen. He liked it better than the
garage. He liked it better than the Parkers'
doghouse. He was happy in the kitchen,
but crowded. The next morning, when he
greeted the Tompkins family, he knocked
over a milk bottle full of milk.

"Never mind," Peter told Mother. "Soon
Leander will have his own special house.
Then he can thump his tail and stretch it out
all the way."

At last, the day after tomorrow came.
When it was late afternoon, Peter and

Leander went out to the front steps and sat there. They were watching for Uncle Jim.

Soon Uncle Jim came up the walk. He had a big roll under his arm.

"Is that the blueprint of Leander's house?" Peter called out.

Uncle Jim nodded. He handed the roll of paper to Peter.

"I can hardly wait to look," Peter said. "But

I think we ought to wait till Daddy comes."

The minute Daddy got home, Peter hurried everyone into the dining room. He was so excited he could hardly unroll the big paper. Uncle Jim helped him. They spread it out on the dining room table, where all of them could see it.

There it was—a blueprint of a doghouse. A most wonderful doghouse! Underneath were these words: A HOUSE FOR LEANDER.

Uncle Jim explained the blueprint to them. There was a big main room. In it Leander

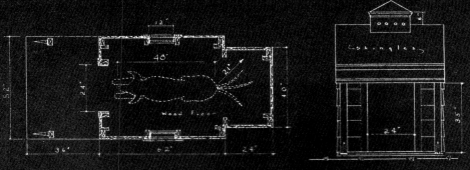

SCALE IN FEET

shingles

TAIL THUMPING
ROOM

35"

Hinge

6" x 6" siding

24"

PORCH
(FOR KEEPING SUN
OUT OF EYES)

12"

7"

12"

40"

24"

2'

40"

Wood Floor

52"

36"

52"

24"

FLOOR PLAN

shingles

24"

35"

FRONT VIEW

A HOUSE ᶠᵒʳ LEANDER

JAMES PERIWINKLE - ARCHITECT & DESIGNER

could stretch out all the way. There was a front porch. This would keep the sun out of Leander's eyes. At the back there was a little room with a low ceiling.

"Here Leander has room to stretch his tail out long," Uncle Jim said. "He can thump it to his heart's content before he goes to sleep. I call this the 'tail-thumping room.'" Uncle Jim grinned.

Peter grinned, too. "He'll like that," he said.

"Give this blueprint to the carpenter who is going to build Leander's house," Uncle Jim told Daddy. "He will know how much lumber to order and how to build the house."

The next day, Peter went with his father to the carpenter's house. The carpenter looked at the blueprint.

"I'll send over the lumber tomorrow," he

said. "The next day, I'll be there to build the house. It will be easy with this plan."

Then he laughed. "First time I ever built a doghouse from an architect's blueprint," he said.

Sure enough, the next day, a truck brought the lumber. And the next morning, the carpenter came.

All day long, Peter and Leander and the Parker twins watched Leander's house as it went up. The carpenter let them hand him

tools. By suppertime, it was finished. "But we must paint it before Leander moves in," said Daddy.

So that night, Leander again slept in the kitchen.

The next morning was Saturday. Daddy did not have to go to the office. He and Peter painted Leander's house. They painted it a pleasant shade of blue.

"That color goes well with Leander's big brown eyes," Mother said.

In the late afternoon, Mr. Flynn stopped to leave Mother a bushel of peaches. Peter took him around to see Leander's house.

"That's the finest doghouse I ever saw," Mr. Flynn declared. "The idea of Leander having a house planned just for him. By an architect, too! Leander's a blessed dog!"

That night again, Uncle Jim had been invited to supper. As soon as they finished their peach ice cream, Peter said, "Come watch Leander try out his new house."

He led the way to the backyard. Mother put Leander's soft old blanket into the new house. They

watched Leander ease himself into the big

room. He stretched out. He put his front
paws out on his front porch. From the room
in the back, they heard his long tail thump,
thump, thumping.

"No more whining at midnight now," said
Daddy.

"No more big dog sleeping in my tiny
kitchen," said Mother.

"No more lonesome dog at night," said
Peter.

Mother and Daddy and Uncle Jim started
back into the house. Peter stayed for a
moment longer. He stooped down and

reached quietly into Leander's house. He rubbed the big dog gently behind his ears.

"I'm glad you're happy in your new house," Peter said softly.

Leander gave a contented sort of sigh. And from the tail-thumping room came the peaceful thump, thump, thump of Leander's long tail.

Check out these other Level 3 books from The Good and the Beautiful Library

Mr. Apple's Family
By Jean McDevitt

The Journey of Ching Lai
By Eleanor Frances Lattimore

New Boy in School
By May Justus

David and the Seagulls
By Marion Downer

goodandbeautiful.com